KUNAL KHUS

The

True

Talisman

BLUEROSE PUBLISHERS
India | U.K.

Copyright © Kunal Khushal Wadgaonkar 2024

All rights reserved by author. No part of this publication may be reproduced, stored in a retrieval system or transmitted in any form or by any means, electronic, mechanical, photocopying, recording or otherwise, without the prior permission of the author. Although every precaution has been taken to verify the accuracy of the information contained herein, the publisher assumes no responsibility for any errors or omissions. No liability is assumed for damages that may result from the use of information contained within.

BlueRose Publishers takes no responsibility for any damages, losses, or liabilities that may arise from the use or misuse of the information, products, or services provided in this publication.

For permissions requests or inquiries regarding this publication, please contact:

BLUEROSE PUBLISHERS
www.BlueRoseONE.com
info@bluerosepublishers.com
+91 8882 898 898
+4407342408967

ISBN: 978-93-6261-546-6

Cover design: Shivam
Typesetting: Namrata Saini

First Edition: June 2024

Contents

1. Beginning 1
2. Fear 17
3. Kingdom of Whia-I 36
4. Kingdom of Whia-II 45
5. Uxbirdland: The Past 60
6. Secrets of Life 71
7. Return of Evil 78

1.

Beginning

It's the month of December. Winter doesn't bother much here in the metropolitan city of Mumbai but yes it gave a glimpse of it these days. Harvey Watson, a 22-year-old guy lived here with his sister named Lily and his grandparents, although they were born in Delhi. The siblings shifted here after the accidental death of their parents. At that time Harvey was just 7. Grandma used to narrate a lot of fictional stories to young Harvey. He was fond of magic and mystery. Even today some of those fictional characters keep running in his mind.

Today, Harvey has a train to board. He wore a bottle green coloured shirt with fine white checks over it and a maritime white coloured bottom. A pair of brown shoes and a rimless frame of specs suit perfectly over him. It's 4 o'clock in the evening and Harvey is accompanied by his two friends, Robert and Rahul. The train usually arrives on platform number 3 so they moved towards that direction.

"So how long is it for the train to arrive?" asked Robert.

"20 minutes more" Harvey replied, checking his watch.

They took the bridge to reach the platform. Coming down by stairs Rahul asked, "Harvey, why are you going to Kolkata all of a sudden? What exactly are you going for and how long will it take to come back?"

"I need to meet my mentor there. I think it will take a few days", Harvey answered, his gaze roaming around to find an empty bench nearby.

"Nice man! It will give you a chance to explore a new city" Robert said and then he pointed towards an empty bench. "Let's sit over there."

The three friends sat on the bench at the platform waiting for the train, reminiscing about the fun they had in their hostel during the bachelor's. Harvey laughed heartily, "Those really were the days guys. We were so carefree, not even a thought of what future holds ahead, living in the present. Live, laugh and enjoy was all we ever did. But see how time has changed." Rahul agreed, "That's the harsh truth of the real world. See how we all are struggling to land a single job. I really wish our lives would always be as simple as it was in the past. But our dear Robert doesn't have to worry about that as he already has a job. Say Robert, how is it going anyway?" Robert chuckled, "nothing much yaar, Naukri ne Naukar bana ke rakha hai. Job is just a beautiful fantasy for outsiders but inside it's just an unending rat race. Speaking of fantasies, Harvey, are you still living in your grandma's old magical fantasy world like you used to tell us the stories back then." Harvey gasped, faking offence "first of all rude! I didn't talk *that* much about it. And second, magic is not just a fantasy, its real", he joked. They all started laughing.

However, they heard an announcement made over the loudspeaker. It informed them about the train that it would be late by a couple of hours than the scheduled time.

Rahul slumped in his seat "I wonder what the issue is." Harvey relaxed beside him. "You were on your way to shopping. You better leave before the stores are closed. I will sit here for a while", he suggested. "You sure? We can wait if you want, no worries", said Rahul. "It's fine you don't need to." Harvey assured.

"Okay then, happy journey. We will take our leave now" Robert got up to bid his goodbye.

"Yup! Thanks once again guys. See you both soon." Harvey said, shaking hands. Then they both started to head towards the station exit "Bring us souvenirs, will you?" Rahul demanded on his way back. Harvey laughed "yeah, yeah I will".

Harvey was sitting alone on the bench now, waiting for the train. He brought out his book and started reading to kill time. Harvey was fond of reading novels. It was quarter to 6 when Harvey received a text from Lily wishing him a happy journey. He smiled and texted her a quick take care message.

After a few minutes, the train arrived. Harvey had a backpack that he took on the shoulder, and a trolley bag that he pulled and boarded the train. He took out the ticket from his wallet to confirm the seat. It was A32. He said to himself, *"Oh wow! A window side seat is the best travel mate"*. He kept his bags in the cabinet and settled down. Then he took out the book from his backpack, turned a few pages, and continued reading from where he left it last time.

The time fled as Harvey got engrossed in his story. He didn't even know when he fell asleep. He was jolted awake by a sound. He looked around, and observed his watch, its 12:45 a.m. Harvey murmured *"I slept for quite a long time huh. Just a few more hours and I will be at my destination"*. Closing his eyes, he tried to sleep but he heard something again. He moved his head up and saw a man taking his suitcase from the cabinet under a dim torch in his other hand. With a big laugh, he opened the suitcase and pulled out a pair of clothes, a blue shirt with yellow round patches on it and a green pants. He also took out his pink-yellow coloured curly hair wig and a pair of shoes. Harvey wondered, *'What is this moron doing at this hour?'*

The man turned his head looked at Harvey and said, "Young boy, my name is Jack and I am a Joker."

Jack laughed hard with his mouth wide open and continued "By the way who are you?"

Harvey's mouth was slack open *'how the hell did he know what I thought? Did he just read my mind? Wait, wait, wait. Did he hear when I called him a moron?'* He was having his inner turmoil but he steadied himself to answer the question "My name is Harvey. I am a student. Can I ask you something? Did you just read my mind or I actually say it loud? I am sorry, I didn't mean that", Harvey said.

"Silly boy. Let that go. Answer me. A student you said. What kind of student are you? Are you a magician in training?" Jack asked. "Never mind" Jack continued without pausing, "let me tell you a joke". And while changing his attire Jack said "What do you call a wolf who lost its pack? A where-wolf" and Jack cracked up hard.

Harvey, who didn't find it funny at all, stared at him, unimpressed thinking why the hell is he dressing up at this point of hour? He asked again, "Well you didn't answer my question, how did you know what I was thinking?"

"Well it's simple, my action at this time... anyone seeing me doing this will think the same way," Jack said. "And this is all because we are about to reach somewhere, our destination you see", he added creating a little bit of suspense.

"Where?" asked Harvey.

Jack interrupted Harvey and said, "Hey I have another joke for you…" Jack was cut off by another voice, "Hey Jack, I told you not to make fun of my adorable cute little pets." a man said.

"whatttt? When did I say anything about your shrimps?" Jack shouted at that man.

The man growled with anger, "Well you always do that! I know you quite well and hey you just called them shrimps, didn't you?"

"I guess you two know each other?" Harvey said.

"So, what!" said Jack while folding his hands with a humph.

The man introduced himself and said, "Hey new fella, I am Big."

Harvey noticed that the man was tall and fat. He had huge muscles, a huge stomach, a blue tee shirt, an old brown leather jacket black muddy trouser a pendant around his neck, and a black beret cap. The Man had huge moustaches that swirl around his cheeks with no beard.

"Yeah, I can see that!" Harvey exclaimed, "I am Harvey by the way. But is that your name for real or something?" he further added.

"Yes, young man, my mom already knew I was gonna be this huge… ha ha ha" Big laughed while patting his belly.

The True Talisman

Jack mischievously asked, "So, Big, where are your little shrimps?"

"You again called them shrimps? Enough of this. I will chop you and feed them I swear", Big said in a loud voice to Jack. He then turned to Harvey "Let me introduce them to you Harvey", he spoke enthusiastically while Jack was still laughing.

The man went a couple of steps to get a few cages from under the seat. In the dim lights, Harvey tried to observe what kind of pets he had in these cages. These were something he had never seen before in reality and couldn't believe his own eyes.

"Well... well... well... these aren't real right? It's impossible" Harvey said, unconvinced. "How could those creatures exist in real life?"

Big had these few creatures that always existed in the stories of his grandmother and he never thought that to be real. "Meet Kerburux" said Big, unaware of Harvey's dilemma, "he is a Cerburus, a species of hound with three heads. He is as tiny as your fist for now but will grow much bigger than us." Harvey got scared to see them as in how a dog-like creature can have three heads. It looked sickening and he couldn't utter any word. *'It's a dream, it's a dream'*, that was all Harvey had in his mind.

"Nah, it's not a dream. Whatever you are seeing is real", Jack casually approached him from the back. Harvey turned around, shell-shocked "Did you actually read my mind? This has happened twice now." Jack laughed hard at his reaction "Nope! That's how people have always reacted when Big showed them his shrimps".

"Next, we have a Wyvern it looks like a dragon but there's a lot of difference between a dragon and a Wyvern. I have named him Yiros" Big added further, ignoring Jack's jab.

"Well, they look cute in this size but at the same time they are quite terrifying. But are they real?" Harvey asked anxiously. Everything was too much to take in for him.

"What do you mean by 'are they REAL'? Of course, they are real. They eat and sleep and poop just like us" Big said light-heartedly.

"When did you guys wake up?" A female voice chimed in interrupting their conversation. Harvey turned around but found no human. Instead, there was a cute little furry animal, a rabbit to be exact, staring at them all with its big, red eyes. Harvey asked Jack, "Who spoke just now? Was it this rabbit?"

"What's making you so doubtful now? Why are you making such a weird face, weirdo? You just saw some creepy creatures and are fine with it but you question me? By the way, my name is Digit and I am a rabbit, a doe to be very specific" Digit said while licking its long ears and continued "And yes of course I can talk! Hey wait, all rabbits can talk. What are you talking about".

"I just never saw one", said Harvey, still in a daze.

"You never saw a rabbit?" Digit interrogated Harvey.

Digit was a white-furred doe. She has a ring-like ornament, golden in colour pierced in her left long ear. "My name's Harvey. And I never met a talking rabbit like you" he said.

Harvey was having a mental breakdown. He has never met such people or had never seen anything like this ever. He had a lot of questions running in his head. *"Is this all real or fake? Some kind of trick or what? Am I dreaming?"* He was blown away by these thoughts. He had no answers to these questions but unexpected happenings were bombarding on him left and right. He was scared and confused. But at the same time, he felt excitement as he was experiencing something for real that had always been the part of his grandmother's tales.

"I came from home. Boarded this train and the train's still moving, the floor's vibrating. I can feel this motion and we are all moving; I can see from the window a few distant lights. Everything's running in the opposite direction. This must be all for real" Harvey reasoned.

"Everyone wake up and get ready we will reach our destination soon" Big shouted joyfully in his loud voice.

Digit hops from one seat to another, on to the people waking them up. "Wake up guys, wake up," she said with enthusiasm. Harvey realized that these people weren't just a few and that the train was full of them. Hustle and bustle started as everyone woke up. Few were cleaning their face with the towels; some started their makeup, while some were changing dresses. Harvey was surrounded by a lot of energetic people, animals, and birds. There were monkeys who were helping others to pass the items. A few children were playing with a white dwarf having long-hair tied in a ponytail. There were beautiful red and green and blue macaws flying freely in whatever space available in their compartment. There were magicians and their co-performers, and many more rabbits and white pigeons also boarded the train.

Harvey also saw that there were other kinds of tiny magical creatures and a couple of them were fighting. They were engaged in the tug-of-war for a small piece of red cloth. One of them fell down and rolled away; the other wrapped the red piece of cloth as a scarf with the proud face of winning. "These are so cute" Harvey laughed. A lady introduced them as raenbug. Raenbugs were small round creatures, brown in color, with heads that looked exactly like mushrooms, with no body and limbs emerging directly from their round head. Big round black eyes that cover a major part of their head make them look really cute.

The lady said, "Raenbugs are the symbol of reality. It keeps the illusions and hallucinations away. Also, they bring happiness and good fortune. And I love these ones very much".

"They look cuter while sleeping. And you know that one? I named it Sleepy; it is quite special. Unlike other raenbugs it sleeps all the time", she said while chuckling.

Harvey said, "They are cute indeed. By the way what's your name ma'am?"

"I am Linda," she replied.

Harvey couldn't help but feel happy and enthusiastic while watching the scene unfold in front of him. He was in awe with everything around, growing curious by every passing minute. He then rushed towards a tiny fairy house kept in the corner over a table. The house was really tiny. Harvey went closer to observe. It had a little mahogany wooden door carved so beautifully in a vintage Italian style, a window closed with little curtains on the inside and clay tiles on the roof. Suddenly the lights of the house were put on and the door opened. A few tiny fairies came out flying. They flew high above Harvey's head. He was amazed and saw them going higher. One of them came flying down and sat on Harvey's shoulder.

"She likes you", said Linda and continued, "These are pixies. Once I was walking through the woods and a bunch of them came out of nowhere and started following me. Since that day we all stay together".

"Do they also signify something like raenbugs?" Harvey asked, totally invested in them.

"Pixies are powerful magical creatures that follow the one they like. You can't run away from them. They always follow you and stay loyal to you. They are good besties. I like them. I guess this one likes you. But each of them only helps you once. After that they disappear", Linda added.

"Oh! Where do they go?" Harvey didn't want them to go anywhere; they had just met after all.

"It is said that they go to their world and sleep and are born again with new powers and they again start searching for someone to fall in love with", Linda answered.

"I am thrilled to meet you all", Harvey whispered to the pixies. "I am thrilled to meet you all really. It is unbelievable but I so want to believe it." Harvey told Linda who just smiled and acknowledged his feelings.

By this time everyone on the train was almost dressed up. Everywhere Harvey looked there was laughter and bright colours surrounded him. It took no time for Harvey to be friends with all the people and creatures he was surrounded with. He sang and laughed and danced with all of them.

"Jack told me there's someone named Harvey with us on the train. He is not one of us and still somehow boarded this train", said a red-toed yellow frog, hopping his way towards Harvey.

"I am Harvey" Harvey answered.

"I am Grogu," the frog said.

"Like a speaking rabbit, like a speaking frog!" Digit exclaimed.

"Come on man! Where are you heading to?" Grogu asked.

"I am going to Kolkata" Harvey replied.

"Kokk... What? Where you said?" Grogu questioned. "The train is moving to Bretford in Empire of Enon".

"NO!" Harvey suddenly remembered his purpose of boarding the train and real-life destination. He started panicking. "What empire? The train is moving to Kolkata. Whatever you are saying seems no logic as such place doesn't exist" Harvey said. The chaos and laughter were silenced in that moment. Everything went quiet.

"That's exactly the place we all belong to Harvey. Big got his shrimps in the form of eggs from the woods of Bretford that later hatched and you met Kerburex and Yiros", Jack said in a serious tone.

"Is this..."

"It's not Harvey. This isn't a lie or a joke. The place you are referring to doesn't exist", Jack said interrupting Harvey.

"No, Bretford doesn't exist. I have never heard of it". Harvey argued

"Harvey, you just witnessed the things you always thought to be imaginary. But they exist. We exist. This train exists and the place exists too", Jack told Harvey.

Linda said, "Listen Harvey I know how you are feeling right now. But believe me and settle down. Let's reach Bretfort first and then from there we will help you to reach Kolkata. At this very moment that's the only option. From the very beginning I knew that you're from a different world and we don't know how you reached here but the way you come to this world is how you will go back to yours. Bretford is our village and there are a few elders who might know what has happened. I guess they might help us with the situation with their experience and knowledge of the strong magical powers they hold."

Harvey wasn't convinced but he calmed himself since he didn't have any other choice. "OK then, I guess I don't have any other option but as soon as we get down from this train, I want you to find me a way to reach Kolkata," he said.

"I believe in destiny. You are here to serve the purpose. Nothing happens without a reason. I am so glad that you have finally arrived" a weak and fragile voice came from a gloomy dark corner of the compartment, startling everyone.

"Do I know you?" Harvey asked as he stepped a little forward to the corner.

Harvey saw an old woman sitting there looking at him. She wore an old pale-yellow gown. She gestured him to come closer. Harvey went to her and observed that the old woman was so weak that her hands were shaking. She could not walk without the help of the staff that she was holding in her hand. She kept that wooden staff inclined to her seat and ran her fingers through her chalk-white hair.

"Do you know him, old lady?" Grogu asked.

"Mm-hmm," the old lady nodded and broke into tears as if her long wait was finally over. She had contentment and happiness in her eyes. "Yes, I know him. He is our savior", she told everyone uttering one word at a time taking pauses while she talked. Harvey didn't understand what she was referring to and he kept looking at the old lady.

"What 'he is our savior' and what will he save us from? I just don't understand a thing. You ignore her

Harvey; she is just an old geezer. She has the habit of saying meaningless stuff no one understands," said Linda ignoring the old lady's words.

At this moment, Harvey and all the others heard some weird noise coming from a distance but approached them with great speed. It was like a deadly scream of animals and humans.

"Did you all hear that? What is that?" There was fear in Big's voice. The situation was getting tensed by the seconds. With each passing moment as the sound was approaching them, it felt like invisible fingers were hovering over their skin making the spines cold.

Raenbugs who sensed the danger jumped over the lap of Linda and they all pushed themselves into her and pixies quickly ran back to their fairy house. Everyone was terrified. With tears rolling down her timeworn cheeks, the old lady shakily whispered, "Time has come."

2.

Fear

The air went heavy and everyone was shaking in their boots. The feeling of terror started growing inside everyone.

"It's so hard to breathe. I am suffocating like my lungs are being crushed; life being squeezed out of me with each breath", Jack shivered in his place. Big nodded "I too feel like my feet are getting numb. I can't even lift a toe." They huddled closer instinctively with the impending horror. Linda leaned towards the window and observed that a big headlight was proceeding towards them with greater speed and the screams were getting louder with each passing moment. She realized there was something evil on that approaching train running parallel to them. "We are gonna die!" she screamed with terror in her eyes. *"It's coming way too fast and we have nowhere to run,"* Harvey thought as he was clueless about the events that were taking place. Running at a greater speed the other train took no time to reach them. Everyone along with Harvey watched those wild, murderous brutes riding over it. They were all over the train not only inside but also on the roof. All the passengers looking at them, terror stabbed their souls, and everyone's faces paled at the horrendous sight in front of them. There were human-like creatures with spears in their hand and featherless wings like a vampire bat. Covered with blood, and dripping from their skin; they seem to be flying directly from hell after a bloodbath. Few were riding dragons. There were two-headed, even three-headed dragons that could breathe fire. There were shape-shifters who had the ability to turn themselves into hungry wolves with large canines and claws. Many venomous snakes also boarded the train. They all with the same hunger attacked Harvey and the others. Screaming and shouting turned all the happiness and fun into fear and turmoil.

Enemies started attacking the train from all directions. Few jumped while the others threw poisonous snakes over them. The few failed to land and died crushing over the railway tracks. Few landed and pounced to behead them. Then the dragons started spitting fire towards the train, the heat melting a few portions of it. This further frightened the already panicked souls and they started running wherever they could inside the train. They were stuck inside it but all they tried was getting away from the attacks to save them but those attempts were up to no avail. The werewolves and vampires forcefully entered the train and started capturing whoever they saw. Big ran to his pets and tried to hide them. Jack went towards the children and others and tried to shift them to other compartments. Harvey was just astounded and conflicted. It was too much to take in. It was gross and frightening. All the enemies were thirsty for blood and flesh. The bright full moon that Harvey was gazing at a moment before was about to turn blood red soon. It was Big whose voice boomed in the compartment bringing everyone to a standstill. "My fellow friends! It is not the time to run. We have nowhere to run any way. But just accepting defeat is worse than death itself. We have the greatest weapon of all- our unity. If we unite our forces, we will all attain victory. If we are facing hell, let's face it head on. So, if you don't wanna die, fight like never before. Fight with every last muscle you have. Use every last magic spell you know. Ensure your survival. I swear to Whia we all will go through this alive. Everyone LIVE!" In that instant, the air shifted dramatically. Now along with fear, there was determination. All the eyes shone brightly with a single aim- to survive and win.

Men gathered all the nearby items that could be used as weapons and some people took the children all the way to the back of the carriage and created magic barrier to shield them. Big himself defended the door and tried to resist the entrance of those enemies. He kicked a few enemies out. However, Big was bitten on his foot by a venomous serpent that appeared out of nowhere. Big wailed in pain but didn't let his guard down.

"Everyone shut down the windows and the doors. Those crawling species are making their way through it" he shouted and continued to defend the entrance of the train. Windows were shut down. Soon Big started experiencing laboured breathing and nausea and it took no time for him to collapse. The other men drew Big back and took his place. Jack, Linda and others were battling those monsters that had entered forcefully, trying to defenestrate them. Suddenly a werewolf attacked Jack from behind, attempting to bite off his neck. Linda hurriedly threw a spell towards them which sent the wolf flying off the train. "Thank you Linda!" Jack appreciated the help. "No problem Jack. Now focus ahead. We have each other's back, yeah guys?" Linda cheered and everyone joined her. Each person was using every ounce of their strength and magic to fight.

"Why am I just looking at others battling? Can I help? Should I help? Will the life of those who just died will go in vain? Are we all going to die? They are all fighting for their survival. They know magic. I have no place in between them. I am trapped somewhere somehow that I don't know. I have no clue. I don't wanna die here" Harvey kept questioning himself while standing at the end of the compartment.

Harvey's stomach churned, acid clawing up his throat. His lungs stopped and the way his heart pounded felt almost bone shattering. Nausea cramped his stomach. He was vaguely aware of what was happening around him. But a certain presence brought him to focus. The old woman held his hand and gazed deep in his eyes. Slowly, he sighed in relief, took a deep breath and forced himself to calm down. *"I am here right now. I cannot just stand like a statue and do nothing. These people need all the help at the moment and I will not be backing down now. I don't have any special powers or magic, but I will do whatever I can to save everyone"*. With no second thought, he ran to grab the cages from underneath the seat and set Kerburux and Yiros free. Both beasts growled and howled, getting gynormous at an alarming rate in no time, they grew enormously, towering over all the passengers, even some deadly villains. They pounced on the enemy, Kerburux ripping off their heads one after another while Yiros feasting on them while climbing on the roof. Everyone, who had felt all doors have been closed, found a gleam of hope shining through the window. Big, who was on the brink of consciousness, had tears of relief in his eyes. All hopeful eyes were in awe watching the creatures in action. "They grew up the size instantaneously that otherwise takes not less than 30 years", Linda said dazed in amazement, "I wonder how this happened". The old woman smiled looking at Harvey, *"We still have hopes with us"*.

Digit was fast and was able to push a few out of the door. Grego helped too. All of them were fighting with their might and capacity. But the sheer number of those monsters was overwhelming. The army of enemies was so huge that even Kerburux and Yiros were unable to survive the battle. How could they? They were mere children after all. They fought till the end, taking multiple of opponents at a time but were eventually overpowered and killed. The numerous spears that pierced their bodies left deep scars in Big's heart as well. "I won't be able to live without them", Big wept in sorrow while cheeks flushed with tears.

"We all gonna die. Just who are they? What do they want from us?" shouted another person. "They all emerged from the dark." The old woman said quietly but it was loud enough that all people surrounding her diverted their attention to her. "They feed on fear and hatred. They feed on humans. They belong to the army of Arwel", the old woman said.

Everyone was stunned and Harvey was no different. He became numb and motionless, unable to absorb anything yet the horror didn't seem to dissipate any time soon. The blood bath occurring around him was unbelievable. *"How can this even be possible? Oh please save us God. Big's creatures died too, what else can we have faith in?"* Harvey was clueless about what do to. *"I am just a normal person, I never believed something like this could even exist and never imagined the things I am witnessing right now."* His mind was reeling, overheating all the same. He was baffled by the situation around when a wrinkled hand reached him.

"We have no time Harvey" the old woman spoke concentrating all her energy and continued "Once we reach Bretfort we all will be safe. You just go and make sure that the train doesn't stop at all. I believe in you, Harvey. What matters today is not the strength of magic but the strength of our will to live on. I believe you can do it. Now go."

Harvey was in no shape to utter a word. Even though he had no idea what he was doing, he just nodded his head and ran through the length of the train as all the compartments were interconnected. Sleepy, the raenbug, and a pixie, mounted on Harvey's shoulder and joined him on the way. Now all he understood was that he had to meet the driver and tell him not to stop the train at any cost. *"Yeah! Everyone is fighting too hard and a lot lost their lives and there's nothing I can do to ensure everyone's or at least my own safety. The old lady has entrusted me. No matter what happens I will contribute my efforts in whatever I can right now"*, Harvey convinced himself, gathering courage in his heart.

Harvey crossed a couple of compartments with blood all over the floor surrounded by part-eaten, distended corpses. He was dodging all the attacks along the way and luckily none were severe enough to compel him to engage in a fight. *"Lucky the compartments here don't have any villains"*, he was relieved. The train was running fast but his heartbeats were faster than never felt before which made the blood rush through his nerves. Harvey single-mindedly kept on running forward. Soon Harvey realized that he had already crossed several compartments but it felt like the train is unending. *"Train can never be this long. Something's happening here. I have never felt so exhausted. Why the heck are my legs trembling and feeling so difficult to raise up"*, he wondered. *"This must be some kind of dark magic of the attackers. Is this the power of our enemies? We are so weak in front of them. How can we survive?"* he said to himself further. All of a sudden, a shape-shifter who jumped over the train lifted a man from the door of the compartment in front of Harvey's and ripped off his stomach to take out the guts and threw him. The creature then went ahead in opposite direction without taking any notice of Harvey's presence. One glance of this incident made a room in Harvey's head. *"I don't want me or anyone be the next one"*, he said, anxious but determined. But Harvey couldn't make it any further. He felt as if he was in no shape to run further. *"It seems that all the energy from my body is drained out. Maybe it is due to the dark magic around. But the old lady has given me her faith. If their lives are in my hand, I will do whatever it takes to save them. I should keep pushing myself ahead, come on"*, Harvey yelled with a confident attitude. Putting one step ahead of the other he started moving up front.

Harvey was too exhausted now. He was unable to take even a single step forward. All the strength lost, he fell on his knees in an empty compartment, heaving and gasping for air. He tried to catch up himself, but felt a movement over the window. He saw a glimpse of something crawling outside the window. Then he heard some footsteps over the roof of the train. Harvey was petrified, both by fear and exhaustion. Instantly, the roof was ripped off and a spine-chilling creature crept inside. He was a human-like creature with sharp canine teeth. He had a tail like a monitor lizard and was full of spikes. Harvey in fright tried to take a step back, but his legs refused to move. The humanoid jumped over Harvey. Harvey closed his eyes and all of a sudden, the creature was thrown away. It was bumped into the wall and fell unconscious. He turned around and found that was the pixie flying around him. Harvey had almost knocked on the door of death and returned "Thank you so much," Harvey thanked his saviour profusely, so glad that he was alive. Pixie couldn't talk but could understand him. It nodded its head with a wide smile on its face. And then it vanished.

"No! Wait. I can't make it without you", Harvey shouted but the pixie was already gone. Harvey stood back on his feet struggling but observed that he could somewhat move and ran from the spot instantly. He again passed a couple of compartments. The moment he put his foot to enter the next compartment everything changed and suddenly he found himself in an open field, a few acres wide. The green grass carpet under his feet was surrounded by a lot of trees. He was stupefied. He looked around bewildered; there were no signs of the train. *"What? The afternoon? The sun's shining so bright here. But it was dark when I was on the train.*

Wait! The train! Where is it? Aren't I in the train? Where am I? I can't feel the movement of the train. The floor isn't moving at all. How can I be here all of a sudden?" He wondered while tapping his feet on the floor to check it. Like he left that world somewhere and now he is in another dimension. *"Another trick! I wonder what else they can do"*, he was beyond frustrated. "Pixie, can you get me out of this place? Pixie?" Harvey tried to call her but no one came "Guess not". At that instant, laughter from a certain direction caught his attention. He noticed that there were a few children playing up ahead. "Hey kids, listen", Harvey called them "Do you have any idea about the train?" The kids shook their heads saying no and then ran away. "Hey wait!", Harvey shouted but none of the children stopped. "Ahh! What the hell is this place now? First the train and now this. I want to get out of here", Harvey tousled his hair in anger while walking straight in the direction boys went.

"No, no, no young man you should not utter such words". Harvey listened to a voice. He looked back and noticed a man coming towards him. The man said, "I have never seen you around here. Tell me, how can I help you?" This man was in his 50s and looked like a farmer as his clothes were soiled and had a bunch of farming tools.

"What is the name of this place?" Harvey asked the man.

"This is a small village named Tupa. And my name is Tuo. You look worried. Can you share with me what's bothering you?" Tuo asked with concerned.

"I am looking for a train and I want to meet the driver", Harvey informed the man.

"A train? There is no train in here. This is a small village. I was born here. Trains don't come here. I have seen trains in cities. By the way, where do you want to go?" the man interrogated.

"How can there be no train? I was just travelling on one! I need to see the driver", Harvey felt a throbbing headache rising by the second.

"Oh! So, you don't want the train. You want to meet someone. Do you know the name of that person?" the man questioned.

"I am not so sure", Harvey said unpleasantly.

"I guess we don't have anyone from our village working as a driver of any train. How are you gonna find him then?" the man asked but continued anyway without waiting for the reply "Don't worry. You look tired, come on let's go to my home. Eat something and we will talk. Also, there you can meet my father. He was a traveller and met a lot of people on his journey. But then old age hit him hard and got settled here. I will be glad if you can get any lead from him", Tuo said cheerfully.

Harvey went with Tuo to his home reluctantly. The house was a small place with dim lights and the walls were patchy with the concrete worn out. The old house had a smell of moist air and a typical smell of animals as there were a few chickens and a couple of goats in the next room.

"Dada, there's someone who wanted to see you", Tuo said to his father.

An old man came out of the door slowly. He was in his 80s may be, had a stick in his hand for support. "Hello, who are you young man and what do you want from me?" he asked.

"Hello Sir, I am looking for a driver of a train. We were over the train and somehow, I got here. I know this may sound weird to you. But that's what happened. And I feel frustrated. All I want is to go back home. I don't know how but I got on the train with different people and then somehow I got here from the middle of my journey", Harvey tried to explain what happened to him but was not sure if the old man can understand him.

"Oh! It all sounds magical", the old man said.

"Yes, there were magical creatures boarded the train. And then we got attacked by unknown people and I was shifted here", Harvey said restlessly.

"Ah! This old age is a curse. I can hardly remember anything these days. But do you know I was born in a kingdom where everyone knew magic? I was a kid and hardly used to understand anything. But as far as I remember, my parents used to perform all sorts of magic", the old man said.

"Oh Dada there you go again", Tuo said to his father exhasperatedly and continued to inform Harvey saying; "he has been telling the same story to me for a long time now. They must be magicians but the ones who perform tricks and create illusions, not the real ones"

The man gave Harvey a glass of water and some jaggery, "Say dada, was they so powerful to convert this glass of water into vodka?" he laughed mockingly. The old man slapped on his son's shoulder "you don't know anything boy and that is why you laugh. I travelled all over the place I could for years back then when I was young. And I found out that this world of ours is a finite cage. No matter what direction we go, though we get to see different villages and cities, and different people of different cultures, but in the end, we always land in the same spot we started from. I travelled to find the village where I was born. But I couldn't".

"What was the name of your village Sir?", Harvey asked curiously.

"I was a kid back then when we left the village. I didn't get to stay there much and don't know the name of the village. Or maybe my parents have told me but I don't remember now", the old man informed sadly.

Harvey asked "When you were traveling..." the old man interrupted him, "I didn't know the name of my village at that time too. But my father told me that the village will always look the same and will never age or change with time. The village was blessed with a divine magical power of its greatest emperor. I always hoped to see it all again, the same way as I left it back then, a place with my childhood memories", the old man said.

"Whatever the old man saying may have some connection with them but everything he is talking about is too vague, making no sense. I still didn't get any lead of how to proceed further. Where to go? What to do?" Harvey was lost in himself.

Tuo said, "Enough Dada, have some rest now" and further brought Harvey back from his stupor, "Harvey it's getting dark already. You can rest here if you want and we can talk tomorrow."

"But there are people on the train who must be worried about me. I won't be able to sleep the whole night. I need to leave from here and reach them", Harvey argued. Tuo placed a hand on his shoulder. "Calm down. I understand you completely. I am sorry as Dada couldn't help you with what you wanted. He spoke everything but told none about the person you wanted to meet."

"Nah! He told me everything he knew. It's just me who couldn't figure out anything yet out of it. I am thankful for whatever your father shared with me", Harvey felt upset but he gave Tuo a small smile. He really was thankful for the old man's help.

"Hey cheer up! I am sure we will figure it out. Have dinner and then we can go for a walk. You can tell me about whatever you have experienced. Your talks are like my Dada. He used to tell me about it but I always thought it was all like a story we narrate to kids. But watching you talking the same... I mean there's something that I don't know about and I am interested in knowing it. Do you adore star gazing? Our village is blessed with a beautiful view. We should definitely go to the fields. Come now let's have dinner", said Tuo to Harvey.

Tuo served rice and beans to his father and Harvey. And everyone started eating. Harvey too had a storm of uncertainties in his mind but in all this fiasco he had forgotten how starved he was. When he saw the served dish and had the first bite, he felt like he hadn't eaten for days.

"Thank you for the food. I really liked it", Harvey said with a smile. Tuo gave him a nod of acknowledgement. "Harvey, you should show us the spot where you landed in our village. Maybe we can get some clues. Maybe I can come with you. I guess my journey is not over yet", Tuo's father suggested Harvey.

After they completed their meal, all three of them walked out of the house as said. Harvey directed them to the same playground where he landed earlier.

"This is where I appeared and saw a bunch of kids playing around here", Harvey said.

"What next? We don't have any clue here", Tuo said to everyone.

"What's that thing over there?", Tuo's father asked with surprise. He pointed at the raenbug who was sleeping while riding on Harvey's shoulder woke up as it sensed the uneasiness in Harvey's mind for a long time now. Even Harvey was startled by his presence. He had totally forgotten about it during this entire ruckus. The raenbug yawned and stretched its tiny arms in the air. Then it moved its two little hands in the air slowly and watched the sky.

Gradually all the clouds floating in the sky descended to the ground making a dense thick sheet of fog that made the surroundings hazy. Harvey couldn't see a thing. He covered his face with the crook of his elbow and saw a blurry appearance of a human coming out of the fog. The fog then disappeared and Harvey found himself in front of the old woman who had arrived. Harvey was joyful to see her as she brought hope to him.

"Let's get out of here Harvey", the old woman said. She tossed her staff twice on the ground and

Harvey found himself back into the compartment of the train.

Harvey held the old lady's hands and expressed his gratitude saying, "Thank you! I thought I would never be able to get out of that place".

"Thank raenbug that helped me to locate you", the old lady said. "Just like Linda told me, raenbugs are the symbol of reality", Harvey said and continued, "So was that a hallucination? I felt everything to be real. I met a few humans there. Was it all fake and all doings of our enemy? Was I over the train all the time? Was I dreaming? I hope this is the reality and not a fake world again", Harvey said.

"Raenbugs Harvey, they only exist in the real world. It's with you now. So, this is reality", the old lady said.

"But it was there in that fake world too", argued Harvey.

"Yeah! But it was sleeping back then. As soon as it woke up, it made sure to bring you back", said the old lady and continued, "Harvey, you have gone through a lot of pressure and that's why you are thinking so much. You need to relax".

"You don't tell that to me. Do you know what I went through? I had a near-death experience. It was the pixie because of whom I am alive. Where were you back then? Why didn't you arrive on time? I can't just stop thinking. It feels like someone is hammering me over my head. I have sadness inside of me as I saw so many of us dying and being eaten up. I have anger for myself since I couldn't do anything. I went mute and stunned to experience all these things. Just what is happening around? I need answers and I know you have them" Harvey said with tears that welled up in his eyes and his throat almost went dry and closed up.

"I will answer all your questions, Harvey. I know you have been going through a lot. But we have very little time, we need to reach Bretford first", the old woman said.

"What Bretford? The train isn't moving to Bretford. I want to go to Kolkata. Just where the hell I am? In what direction the train is moving? I am unwillingly stuck with you" said Harvey crashing all his anger over the old woman.

"Nothing happens without a reason, you are our savior", the old woman said.

"Do you know what I saw right there? I saw massacre, and bloodshed, and went over innumerable corpses. What savior? Who is the savior? I have nothing to do with all of this. Just where am I?" Harvey kept asking questions.

"I don't know about your origin and how you ended up here. But as I already told you, everything happens for a reason. Here in this world, you are the inherent of chronokinesis. You can change the time.

What do you think about how Kerburux and Yiros grew in an instant? It was you. Unknowingly may be, but you did that. Listen, Harvey, I have very little energy left in me and I am counting my remaining days. I will die soon. But before that, I will answer all your questions", the old woman said.

The old woman gathered every last ounce of her energy and took Harvey somewhere else as she tossed her staff twice again on the floor of the train.

The surroundings changed, as Harvey found himself standing with the woman at the banks of a river. Everything around him was moving way too slowly than normal. The wind blew slowly and dried leaves fell from the tree but touched the ground sluggishly. Harvey also noticed the birds flying in the sky were moving at a very low pace.

Harvey was dumbfounded and asked, "Where are we? What is this place?"

"Don't worry; you are in my elemental space. Time moves slowly here and everything in the outside world is paused. I am weak enough that I could not use this power again", the old woman answered and continued, "You see the river, this is River Musa, a place where Arwel was born. Arwel... the word that stands for destruction. But before that let me tell you about the Kingdom of Whia".

3.

Kingdom of Whia - I

The old woman narrated the story, "The magnificent kingdom that spread across the seas covering hundreds of thousands of villages, towns, and cities was known for its very skilled administration, prosperity, and happiness. The great Kingdom of Whia was renowned for its unparalleled strength, unwavering loyalty, and kind and friendly leadership. It was a land covered with mystique and wealth.

The kingdom boasted an army with innumerable cavalry, chariots, infantry, and hoplite soldiers; known for their battle tactics and bravery, that used to strike fear straight into the hearts of their adversaries. The silver shining armour coupled with the double-edged swords made these warriors highly skilful in combat. Not only that these warriors instilled with an unbreakable sense of commitment towards the throne but also, they considered it as a devotion to their deity, a sacred thing as they protected their people and its realm.

At the helm of this mighty kingdom stood King Theo Orabelle, a wise and just ruler who held the respect and admiration of his people. He was known for his fairness and he ruled with an open heart, always putting the needs of the people first. Theo was a man with undying devotion to the deity. He was also an exceptional researcher and had a great knowledge of medicine, administration, politics, and leadership. He possessed a rare ability to anticipate the concerns of the needy, their hopes and dreams and he effortlessly used to weave their ambitions to the welfare and development of the nation.

Theo Orabelle was a man with a dream of conquering the whole world. His desire to capture each and every land was so intense that it was nearly impossible for enemies to put an end to his fearlessness. Theo Orabelle's power was limitless. No one knew the source of his power. Rumors spread across the land; some said he had a special blood trait that is the source of his power as that is something that comes from within, while others said he was a devil that had landed straight from hell.

But the truth was he was the possessor of Talisman. A Talisman is an object that can take any form and has magical powers stored in it. Talisman follows each member of Orabelle's family right after they are born and appears only when they become worthy of it. It is said Theo once destroyed a whole village with just one blow of his Morbid blade, a sword that was said to be gifted to him by the core of Earth itself. The Morbid blade was Theo's Talisman.

Theo was a man of honour, a friend for a friend, and a foe for a foe. No one was as great as him when it came to serving his own people. The care for its people went far beyond the walls of the castle. Theo used to welcome and treat all the lives with dignity whether rich or poor. "Need drives man to action. Action should always be for the benefit of people surrounding us" he always used to say. He not only ruled the kingdom but was ruling the hearts of his people. A king who never hesitated to labour in fields, who never hesitated to swallow the bit of food from the hands of farmers. "To uplift their lives, I should first learn to live like them," he was indeed an ideal emperor.

Whia became a safe haven where compassion and empathy triumphed over prejudice and discrimination. Within the nation, the people thrived in a great way of life. The colourful market stalls hummed with the energy of vibrant trade and the mingling of diverse cultures. The kingdom's economy flourished, thanks to the beloved king's progressive policies and commitment to fair trade practices.

The greatness of the Kingdom was not only due to these physical attributes but also due to its intangible qualities. The people of Whia were bound together with a great sense of unity, an unspoken promise to be there for those who seek help, and a deep respect for each other's differences.

The Kingdom of Whia fortified by Theo became a prime example of compassion and greatness that exist when the ruler and its people are in perfect harmony.

Theo was a great leader, a great king, and a great father. Theo had two sons Eldrian Orabelle and the younger one was Ezra Orabelle. The community embraced both the princes. During their birth, both times it was the same dark night due to no moon and the people lighted rows of candles all over the land to celebrate the moment. To mark these days every year the whole land used to be lit so as to spread the message that Whia will exist forever under the same reign of the Orabelle dynasty.

Both the brothers, Eldrian and Ezra were reflections of their father Theo Orabelle. Both were adept in terms of their physical strength, magical powers, or their intelligence in understanding political administration, literature, or combat skills. They both became worthy and their Talismans accepted them at a very young age.

However, siblings share genes, not personalities. Both brothers shared similar height and weight, the same hair colour, and the same family name. However, there were certain things that made both the brothers different than each other. Eldrian was bold and brave. He was sure that as he was older, he would be the next ruler. He already owned everything, born into a prestigious family where everyone respected him as a prince, a huge kingdom, and a huge army who were loyal to their kingdom and ensured the safety of the people. He was the one who used to love handling things on his own without anyone's interruption, which made him arrogant. But Ezra was quite different. He was kind, helpful, and generous. He valued every person in the kingdom saying everyone has a role here and plays an important part in making the Kingdom the Kingdom of Whia.

There were many incidences that occurred between the two brothers, one to mention was the day when Eldrian being proud of his wealth dared Ezra to set an Oralle on fire. Ezra denied saying, "Even if it is just one Oralle it takes a lot to earn it. You can do so much with this. You can buy food to eat. There are poor who earn that amount over a whole day of work". Eldrian ignored and burnt an Oralle. "We already have a lot and we have the potential to create more. I believe in my strength. Why to worry Ezra?" Eldrian argued. This and many more incidences were all observed by Theo.

Soon Theo was diagnosed with a chronic disorder and there wasn't much time left. The kingdom needed a new emperor. A ruler who rightly can take the place of Theo himself. Finally, the day arrived, the blackest day in the history of the Kingdom of Whia. Theo called both of his children to his deathbed. Both brothers were sad seeing the condition of their father. It was raining outside as if even the sky couldn't see

The True Talisman

Theo's situation. Theo extended his both hands to hold his children and asked them for a promise. "Whatever you ask us for Father, we are ready to do it", said Eldrian confident that he was the next one to ascend the throne. However, things didn't work according to Eldrian. Theo asked Ezra to be the King and to take his place and Eldrian was made Ezra's chief advisor. Theo did what he found the most appropriate course of action and he thought that this decision would ensure Whia's good fortune.

Eldrian left the room without asking a question with a bad temper as his all dreams were shattered. "An advisor, that too for my younger brother and he will be the next King. Is that a joke Father?" Eldrian murmured and continued, "He is no comparison to me. He is weak and a coward. How does he even has a chance?"

Soon after that, Theo died. But right before his heart stopped, he blessed all the people of the Kingdom of Whia and since then everyone who is born in the kingdom knows little magic though they lacked any power like the Talisman. "Regardless of time, the kingdom will remain the same forever. The kingdom is my responsibility and even death can't stop me from my duties. I will be reborn to ensure its safety". These were Theo's last words.

After the cremation, a heavy veil of sorrow hung over Whia's land and the hearts of every being. But the time never stops for anyone. As said, the throne was ascended by Ezra. It took no time for Ezra Orabelle to prove that he was the mirror image of Theo. The new ruler was renowned for his kind and helpful behavior. The people accepted him and everything was flourishing well under his shadow.

But not everyone was joyful. It is said that you never reap delicious fruits if you plant spikes. These spikes were planted inside Eldrian and that ignited the feeling of hatred and anger".

Harvey was listening to the old lady carefully but was irritated and asked "But who is this Arwel and why did he attack us? And what does he have to do with the story of Orabelle you just told me" Harvey asked.

The old lady replied, "I am Reva Orabelle, Queen of the Kingdom of Whia, daughter of Ezra, and granddaughter of Theo Orabelle."

Harvey was surprised. His eyes were wide open as if he could have never imagined that the old woman who was so weak and who was traveling with him on the train could be a Queen of some land.

"But then what happened to the Kingdom? Where are your People?" Harvey asked.

"It all vanished and all that was left behind was smoke, crying, and misery. All we heard earlier were the rumors of Arwel that he is someone who was born from the darkness. He has a never-ending thirst for

The True Talisman

blood and flesh. He crushes human lives for his pleasure. He has a huge army of demons who can wipe out an entire village in minutes with a single gesture from him. We believed these rumors on that black day when Arwel arrived in our Kingdom with his army as huge as thrice what we ever had. His presence was evil, the dark clouds surrounded the sky, and all the flowers, fruits, and leaves on the trees started to dry and fall. The trees died as if their souls were sucked out. The air went stuffy and oppressive. We tried to resist and tried to ensure safety but all attempts led to failure. The demonic army Arwel brought with him ate our people. All left behind were tears, sadness, and sorrow. Arwel killed my lover and a child I was carrying inside of me. The Kingdom was torn off, shattered into pieces. He took everything I ever lived for. We were the few lefts after that time. Just a bunch of people you already met. Our clan was destroyed. We now are nothing more than travellers who pay visits to different villages showing certain magic tricks to earn a few- enough to feed us all", Reva told Harvey.

Soon Reva felt weak, and started coughing and her spell vanished bringing Harvey and her back to the train from the elemental space. Harvey helped her to rest along the seat, "but why did Arwel launched his attack on Whia in the first place? I can't understand it. How come he randomly targets a kingdom he has no connection to?" Harvey's mind was even more muddled after hearing the story. Reva sighed "he didn't have any connection with Whia that is correct. But he wasn't the only one behind the assault. The real mastermind orchestrating this onslaught was none other than my own uncle, Eldrian.

4.

Kingdom of Whia-II

Harvey was astounded by the revelation, "how is this even possible? I understand that he was not happy with Theo's decision but he was the Prince of Whia right? Why would he go against his own land? And how can someone do destruction of this level?" Reva gestured Harvey "Come sit here", she then continued, "I completely understand your confusion in this regard. There is a story behind that but it may take some time. Do you still wish to hear it?" Harvey nodded "I think I should know all the details if we are now facing the enemy head on." "Alright then. Let me tell you the tale of Eldrian"

A few years before the death of King Theo Orabelle, both the princes were married to the princesses of a neighbouring Kingdom of Uxbirdland. Prince Eldrian was married to the elder Princess Aria and Prince Ezra married to her younger sister Princess Liona. The grand wedding ceremony was celebrated in both the countries with extravagant festivities. The land was filled with more joy with bright hopes for the future after a few months when the news was announced that Prince Ezra and Princess Liona were expecting their first baby. Eldrian felt envious about it since it was the matter of the future heir to the throne but he was happy for his brother none the less, since he was confident enough that he will be declared as the crown prince of Whia, and his children will have the first right to ascend the throne despite their age. But soon the desolate news of King Theo's illness led to the selection of Prince Ezra as the Crown Prince of Whia.

Prince Eldrian was devastated by the decision. He argued with his father but it was futile. His decision was final and no amount of persuasion would make him alter it. Eventually, Eldrian swallowed the bitter bullet and became the chief advisor to the then King Ezra after King Theo's demise. He performed his duties duly but felt humiliated everyday even by entering the throne room. *'The throne belongs to me, Whia belongs to me. I should have been the King not him'* he tried to keep such thoughts away but they still haunted him. He spent sleepless nights, his relation with his wife deteriorated day by day. He distanced himself from others and started wandering off in the middle of the night. On one such night, he went in the royal library to spend some time. He was exploring the place and went deep inside. He never went that far since he never needed to. He went to the last of the racks and took out some books. There were some books he had never seen before. He then pulled another one but suddenly the floor beside him began to shake. Eldrian was shocked to see a hidden door opened in the floor beside him he was unaware of. Curiously, he followed the path downstairs. It was too dark to see anything clearly but some traces of magic were present. As he went further inside the lights around him magically turned on along with his movement. He then reached a centre chamber which was surrounded by various books, equipment and potion vials. At the very centre of the chamber, there was an altar like structure with some engravings on the floor. All this was spooky but it piqued Eldrian's interest. It didn't take him long to figure out why the place was kept a secret. It was the epicentre of dark magic. *'Who must have built this?'*, he wondered. It was the ancestorial secrets of Talisman's other side. But instead of informing anyone about this, Eldrian was drawn to the chamber every night. The desire to become the King became strong every day. He knew his brother was at par with him in each parameter. Hence, he needed something more powerful to win. The dark chamber gave him that hope of victory.

In this way, Eldrian dedicated himself to encompass the study of dark magic. He did not spare even a single night and continuously concentrated on honing his skills. In this process, he had exchanged his soul for the demonic power and has become evil himself, but no one could tell since he never let anyone know. On the outside he performed all his duties towards the King and the country, but in hindsight, he started forming his dark army to take over the nation someday. King Ezra had no clue and kept his utmost trust on his chief advisor.

One night when Eldrian was immersed in his dark meditation, the foul energy around him began to emit in all directions. It was immiscible to all but some strong magic wielders could still feel it. Like King Ezra. He woke up with the feeling of unease and sensed the dark energy. He started following it which eventually led to the dark altar. Ezra was flabbergasted to see his own brother in the middle of a ritual circle, surrounded by dark matter and red flames of dark magic. "Elder brother! What are you doing? What is the meaning of all this?" he shouted which broke Eldrian's focus. He opened his eyes and saw his younger brother all messed up. "Oh, it's you Ezra. I am surprised to see you here. Well, the cat is out of the bag, I guess. But I can't let it go any further now, can I?"

Eldrian raised his arm in front when thunder roared out of nowhere and his Talisman- a Trident appeared in his hand. Without wasting a moment, he launched his attack towards Ezra. Ezra being defenceless and confused went flying due to the impact with a bang. Eldrian approached in his direction. Ezra winced but got up "Brother! Why are you doing all this? What has happened to you? You are attacking your own brother now! I don't understand any of this. Please stop this and talk to me I beg you". Ezra tried to reason with him. Eldrian laughed out loud mockingly. "Talk! What has remained to talk Ezra? You have gotten everything, throne, kingdom, power all of it! All of it which was mine! Mine from the beginning and all of a sudden everything mine was ripped off of me and given to you". Eldrian's voice soared around. He sent another attack flying in the direction of Ezra. Ezra defended himself with his magic. "Throne? Kingdom? Power? Oh, brother I never asked for any of this. I was always happy just to be your younger brother following you. I just wanted to fulfil our father's last wish. You could just have asked brother and I would have given up all of it to you." Eldrian scoffed "One never needs to ask for what is their own! The throne belongs to me. I am the elder son. You want to humiliate me by giving the kingship to me in pity?" Eldrian attacked Ezra with full force. "Father was wrong but now I will correct it. I can take what is mine with my own power. Magic is magic, dark or not it is just a means to be powerful and now I am powerful to take you down. I will be the new Emperor!" Ezra protected himself and once again tried to subdue Eldrian's insanity, "Brother you need to stop. This is not the way to settle this. You will destroy everything". "Let it be destroyed then! I will rebuild my kingdom in my own way", Eldrian was so power drunk all the other matters became useless for him. "I didn't wish to fight you but you leave me no choice brother. I, being the king, will protect my kingdom and people whoever I may be standing against. I will stop you right here, even if it means I will have to kill my own brother" Eldrian snickered "you think you can kill me?? Win against me? So ambitious little brother. I am stronger than you and have attained humongous amounts of power in this small period of time. You don't stand a chance" Eldrian fired his dark magic to Ezra. Ezra, now determined created a shield with his own magic. The two powerful attacks collided with blinding light, destroying the fort's wall. When it settled, Ezra's Talisman, sword and shield, donned his armour. All this fiasco alerted everyone in the fort and the capital city. The queens and princess came running to the spot and were horrified to witness the scene. Even the citizens gathered around to see what caused these earth-shattering noise.

The two brothers back and forth numerous attacks. Eldrian was very powerful in his own right but relied only on his magic. But Ezra has true purpose to fight that was to protect his people and also to bring back his brother on the right path. He had perseverance to stay determined in the war. The spectators were in awe and perplexed to see the two brothers fighting who were the epitomes of brotherhood. Ezra then noticed the people around and decided to take the fight somewhere else to reduce destruction any further. He slammed his sword to the ground and soared in the air. He started flying in the direction of the seashore.

"Running away Ezra? Why being coward all of a sudden? Come back and face me like a true King!"

The True Talisman

Ezra ignored him and reached the seashore. "You will not hurt anything else here brother Eldrian. You are going down here. I request you, stop this now otherwise I will reluctantly have to stop you by force". "You are not capable of stopping me by any chance Ezra! I will defeat you and become the ultimate ruler of Whia".

The epic battle of Eldrian and Ezra continued for approximately two days nonstop. At the dusk of the another day both were completely exhausted. Their magic was dying down but going on sheer fumes, not ready to back down. Eldrian then created a black ball of dark matter in his palm with his remnants of magic and threw it on the ground. It blasted expelling black smoke surrounding both of them. No one could see a thing but Eldrian caught sight of his little brother and dashed in that direction. In one swift motion he stabbed Ezra with his trident, causing Ezra to howl in pain. Eldrian tired but finally happy with his victory taunted Ezra "I win Ezra. I told you right? You are no match to me. I am the true worthy king. Now go join our father in afterlife". But a jolting pain sneered Eldrian with shock. He then saw the stabbed figure in front of him melted. A voice behind him startled him. "You are drunk on you power and green Eldrian. But your over confidence and ill intentions are the cause of your downfall" Ezra had stabbed him with his sword in the gut. "Please stop now. Hope you find you peace in your afterlife", Ezra released his sword, causing Eldrian to fall down face first on the ground. Ezra, tired and weak, started going towards the city. He was exhausted, both physically and mentally broken inside due to loss of his brother. Suddenly something hit him making him fall. Wincing, he turned around to see his wounded brother smirking. "You let your guard down at the end. If I am going down, I will take you with me. I have cursed you, Ezra! You will not live long. You will die very soon. If I don't get the kingdom, you will not get it either. Die a painful death!" with these words he collapsed.

Ezra, not dead but feeling almost dying, crawled towards the fort to ensure people's safety. But the soldiers soon found their king and took him back to the fort safely. Even in exhaustion Ezra announced and explained the complete reality to his citizens. "My fellow Whia citizens, it was unfortunate that all this has happened. My brother Eldrian was involved in certain magical malpractices that I believed to be harmful to our Kingdom. As a king I performed my duties. And now I assure you the peace of Whia is safe. I hope you put your faith in me and I will strive to maintain the peace and valour of Whia". People cheered happily praising their king. Everyone easily neglected the evil lord Eldrian who, unconscious, was swept away with the waves into the sea".

Reva continued, "When my father regained his consciousness after the battle, along with relief of his wellbeing, there was grief and sorrow due to the unprecedented turn of events. The loss and treachery of the elder prince added with the sublime health of the current King influenced the trust of the citizens in the royal family. Father recovered slowly but the mental and physical impact ran deep within him, which led his condition to plummet. Numerous healers from Whia and around the neighbourhood kingdoms diagnosed his condition but to no avail. In the end, elder healer concluded that the king was suffering due to a dark magic curse which was absorbing his life energy slowly but still at an alarming rate. It meant that he will die in the near future. The news left us devastated but mother decided it was in the best interest to keep it hidden. And soon, that black day came. The great kingdom of Whia immersed in immense grief with the loss of another great emperor of all times. My mother then ruled the Kingdom of Whia; tried to stand once again as strong as it could.

As it is said, time stops for no one. It heals even the deepest of wounds but the scars may remain. Those grim times passed. After 15 years, I ascended the throne as the queen of Whia along with my husband, and my people welcomed us with open arms. With all my strength and capability, I let my country for several years. When it seemed that the Kingdom was now at peace and the looming shadows of pain started to fade, Arwel attacked us with his enormous army when we least expected it. Arwel's army was ruthless, killing anyone in sight and obliterating everything surrounding them. The destruction was borderline genocide and I was unable to save my people, including my husband and our unborn child. God knows how I survived along with a handful of children surrounded by wreck and ruins. Stuck between a rock and a hard place, we all fled our own land with a heavy heart. Our only option was to seek refuge from Uxbirdland but when we had just reached at the border, we saw demons of Arwel's army guarding the perimeter.

Arwel had taken over Uxbirdland as well which shattered the only ray of hope we had. Helplessly, we had to travel from one village to another in order to survive. It also facilitated us to hide from Arwel as he was still searching for us. It's been decades now. The children I took with me are all grown-ups now. To meet our ends, we performed as street magicians, entertaining the locals with simple magic tricks. We just wanted to live our lives with whatever we could have. We somehow managed to sustain till now but after all these years, history is repeating itself." Reva wiped the tears flowing from her worn eyes. "I still can't comprehend what it is that Arwel wants from us but one thing is certain- this attack will lead to loss of every innocent life on this train and more if Arwel is not stopped right here. I have lost my family, my land, people once before. I won't let it happen to us again. Harvey," Reva raised her hand towards him," I know I am feeble and in no condition to back such brave statements, and I understand it is a lot to ask of you, but will you help me child? Will you support me to save my loved ones and my legacy?"

"I now know about Arwel and I am well aware of how strong he is. But I promise you I won't stop. I understand I am not capable to fight him but the fight is still going on and I need to reach to driver. I will give it my all", Harvey reassured Reva as well as himself. He left Reva and went ahead in the direction of the engine. Eventually, he reached that compartment of the train where the driver could be found. He was merely a couple of inches away from the door. His nervousness caught on him he felt nauseated, a hoard of thoughts invading his head-space. *"Is the driver dead or alive? Are there any enemies behind this door? Will I stay alive at this point or will I be dead?"* Harvey was now scared of what he learned about Arwel but he was privy to the responsibility on his shoulders.

He gathered his courage and extended his sweaty palm to the knob of the door. The moment he touches it, everything disappeared. The door vanished; the compartment and the whole train itself vanished. Instead, he found himself straight into the depths of hell. He also noticed that the whole surrounding was fiery and rivers of lava flowing around him. He looked up and he found himself into the epicentre of that purgatory surrounded by cliffs and valleys from all sides. Then he heard the roars and the screams echoing across the area. Harvey was terror-struck deep into his spine. He saw that there were those wolves and humanoids encircling him, there were wyverns flying around in the sky ready to scavenge him any time. He felt bewildered about the sudden happenings but he had no time to dwell on it since he was all alone, cornered from all directions.

All of a sudden, he felt certain heaviness in the air; it was suffocating like all the air around was sucked. A huge red horn-headed dragon majestically glided down towards the land. When it landed with the gust of the dragon's wings, the ash on the ground dispersed in the air blocking the vision and making the scene blurry. Harvey shielded his eyes with his forearm and when the dust settled, he opened his eyes to see a man getting off the back of the dragon. The giant armoured man towered over Harvey.

Undoubtedly that man was Arwel. He resembled with the imagery Harvey had formed about him according to Reva's description. The menacing aura radiated from his all physique, enough to intimidate anyone in a single stare. He was confident that he was in front of Arwel. When Arwel reached at the arm's length of Harvey, the latter was shaking in his boots. His heartbeat accelerated at an alarming rate, his heart threatening to burst out of his ribcage. His mind was puzzled dumb and with eyes, comically wide, he just stared at the mountainous being standing in front of him.

"Who are you?" Arwel growled with a rough voice. He lifted his shadow-fang blade up in the sky. A stream of fire landed from the night sky over his weapon and now it was blazing red. "I shall kill you," Arwel said monotonously as if killing was his second nature. All the demonic creatures surrounding the cliff started howling, and screeching.

Words were stuck at Harvey's tongue and didn't dare to come out. He took a couple of steps back fearfully to avoid the attack which made Arwel laugh. "You are a mere powerless human. You are weak. You are helpless. All you have always known is whine and shed unnecessary tears when you don't get things you desire. You should dare to snatch for what belongs to you but humans... just can't do that. Pathetic! You are like an insect to me. A worm that lives a very short life in a confined space". Arwel said pointing his blade toward Harvey.

Arwel then gestured with his other hand and a couple of demons brought over a cage containing unconscious bodies of friends of Harvey all tied up. "Here, see that? This is what happens when you just don't accept death and dare to fight back your destiny. See them, boy. Can they still be recognized?" Arwel guffawed like a maniac, hatred and cruelty evident on his face.

Big, who was bitten by a venomous snake was already dead and Linda had lost all her Raenbugs. Jack was in rough shape. The poor pixies had their wings clipped off and couldn't even move.

Seeing this Harvey was flabbergasted but the same time, his anger reached at its peak. Despite of knowing that he has no chance to confront Arwel he stood for his friends. *"I am alive because of them. These demons have destroyed the homes of thousands of villagers. These are the ones responsible for Reva's condition and the death of several of my friends. How can someone be so heartless?"*

He squared his shoulders and looked at Arwel straight in his eyes, "Arwel, humans are built like this. We cry when we see others in pain. We stand by the side of people we love. These are the emotions that make us human. If you don't understand the meaning, I doubt you are even a human Arwel"

"Arwel? Oh yeah, that's what everyone started calling me. I don't even remember when Satra became Arwel. But you are right. I am not a human. I don't consider myself as one of you wimpy creatures. I am a monster created by wrong doings of humans themselves. My ultimate goal is to destroy each and every person belonging to the Kingdom of Whia", Arwel declared.

"Why? Why are you so fixated? What did they do to you? It was you who eliminated thousands of homes and committed genocide on the land of Whia", Harvey argued.

Arwel laughed, "Oh! So, you know the tale! I don't care what you think about me, I can rip you apart right now. But, before that, I want to appreciate you. You have some guts to question me. Rather you are the first I ever met who opened his mouth to speak; everyone else opened their mouth just to scream and beg for mercy facing me" Arwel scoffed, "You know nothing of the past yet you got some nerve huh! Let me tell you about Satra that became Arwel."

5.

Uxbirdland: The Past

Tsesesam was a small village in Uxbirdland where the Kamusa tribe resided. The word Kamusa refers to the people living on the banks of river Musa. I belonged to that tribe. I lost my mother the day me and my twin sister were born. Our family was poor. Our father used to travel a long way for his work just for meagre wages which were insufficient to meet our needs. There were times when we had no food and had to sleep hungry. Our home was old and broken, water dripping from the roof during monsoon. We were deprived of food, motherhood, and received nearly no love from our father. *"Why were we born to such a family?"*, I always used to wonder. Some villagers used to call me and my sister demons who ate our own mother. Hardships, pain, and suffering were the part of my life since the childhood. The only light in my gloomy life was my beautiful sister, Dhansiri. Her deep brown eyes used to sparkle whenever she smiled, her smile rivalling the sun itself. She was the only symbol of hope, happiness, and contentment for me and I had promised myself to dedicate my entire life to her. When it comes to the people you truly care about, you don't really worry about yourself. "God if you really exist. I just wanna pray that I don't need anything else. I have my sister, it's more than enough and I don't want anything more but please don't take anything from us either. I beg you. Please God!" I always used to pray.

One day, an announcement was made all over our village informing about the group of people who would be arriving for their magical performance on the occasion of some royal celebrations. Dhansiri was over the moon when she got to know about it and pleaded me to take her to attend the show.

"It will be so fun, won't it Satra? I am very excited to see them perform. I have heard countless stories regarding their tricks. Some say they could even turn a piece of paper into a white pigeon or a rabbit. I will watch them and learn from them. We are going Satra, aren't we?", Dhansiri said and continued "It is the first time such kind of crew is visiting our village. Who knows when will we get another chance to see something like this?".

"You aren't well Dhansiri. You are already suffering from fever since last few days. You should rest. I will definitely take you to see it whenever they will visit our village next time", I told her.

"But it is magic Satra! I have never seen it before and such opportunity is so rare to find. Now that it is on our doorstep why waste it? I wonder if we will ever get another chance. The whole village will be there. I wanna be there too", Dhansiri kept arguing.

I opened my mouth to convince her but she denied listening to me. "I will be happy watching them. Happiness is all that we ever wanted, isn't it Satra?"

My heart melted due to her words. I could do anything for her happiness. Hence, we went that evening.

There were men and women performers, dressed in colourful vibrant clothes showing off their impeccable performances with great enthusiasm. Many magical creatures that I had never seen or believed could exist also took part in some tricks. All the villagers assembled and surrounded the stage. We were also a part of that huge crowd. I was so happy. But the major source of my happiness was watching my little sister laughing and cheering heartily. She looked so adorable that evening.

But she was ill and exhausted. All of a sudden, she fell unconscious. I saw her collapse right in front of me. It made me horrified.

"Dhansiri, wake up. What happened to you? You were just smiling a minute ago... Dhansiri... Dhansiri...." I was so panicked. Other people around were so spell bound in the performance, they were completely unaware of our situation. I went to other people and asked them for help. I went to each and every person I could.

"Please. please.. Someone please help me" I kept shouting with tears welling up in my eyes. "My sister there needs help. She has fainted please help us."

No one came. They even pushed me away. Everyone was so busy with their own happiness that they denied seeing my pain. Everyone seemed to forget that in the end, I am also a human, just like them.

I came back to my sister crawling on the ground to find her still. I shook her to wake her "Dhansiri wake up please. I will take you somewhere else..." But my words were futile. Her breathing had already stopped. I had lost the only person dear to me. Everything went blank. I became deaf to the music and fun coming from the performance. I became deaf to the people enjoying.

Silently, I took her away from that ominous place to our home. I sobbed loudly, "Why? Why this injustice, God? You created all equally but why there is only pain and misery in our fate? Why don't others help us? It just doesn't matter anymore. Happiness is just a myth those performers cast upon us. Just a false feeling that everyone thought was more important than my sister. I hated them so much. Tonight, I lost my world. All I have now are memories. So, little I lived my life with her. Dhansiri's soul was snatched by those magicians. My only regret is that I wasn't there around her when she was on the verge of her death. Without Dhansiri nothing here is worth living. Without her, I am nothing."

With no set path I left home. I never liked or felt any connection with the place I grew up. Soon I forgot what was home like and I stayed in the woods on the outskirts of Uxbirdland. I believed that I was made to live alone, waiting for my demise.

In the woods, the only companion I had was the setting sun. A beautiful burning ball of fire that exactly resembles my heart. Every day I used to travel across forest to reach to the seashore. There I watched the setting sun slowly descending into the ocean, engulfing the world into the darkness. It truly was a mirror to the state of my heart. Yet the sinking feeling never ceased to be. I just used to observe it blankly. Time passed and I lost count of the days since I started living there in the woods. One evening when I was on my way back under the moonlight, to my shelter, I found a middle-aged man with patchy old clothes on the side of the ocean. He was sitting there facing the shore looking at the water.

"Hey! Who are you? What are you doing down there? Go away from this place" I shouted. I had seen a human after a long time and the anger rushed into my veins and all over my body. I just could not withstand the presence of humans around me. My spine got cold.

Even the sight of a human reignited the old wounds of pain and loss of Dhansiri.

The man turned around to see me. "I am on my way back", the man raised both his hands in submission to calm me down. He then stood up and started limping in other direction.

He went. I came back to my place. I fired the woods for light. Then I sat on the ground and cooked some rice to eat with jaggery. Suddenly, I heard the rustling sound of something passing through the dense foliage. I had stayed in the forest long enough that these typical sounds didn't scare me anymore. I turned around to take a look in anticipation of any wild animal. But I saw the same man who came following me.

"You again?" I was enraged. *"Why even this human was following me?"*

He swayed his right hand gently and suddenly with the movement of his hand, the bonfire was out. It was all dark that I could not see a thing. And after a moment he rekindled it all again with the same motion of hand.

I was astounded with the whole ordeal. I was at a loss of words since I had never seen something which seemed like magic so up close. My state of dumbstruck gave him the opportunity to speak. "Who are you? What's your name and why do you stay here in the forest?" he enquired.

"My name? My name is Satra. But it doesn't matter anymore. It's been a long time since someone has called me by my name. I have no one with me". I told him making it sound nonchalant but the look in the man's eyes said otherwise.

"My name is Eldrian," the man said. "I am a traveller" he added further. This was the first time when I observed him thoroughly. He was in a bad shape, looking severely injured and exhausted. I spoke nothing so he continued "I also don't have any home to return to now". The man sat beside me "This is my first ever journey on my own".

"Why? Are you looking for something?" I asked him.

He smiled looking at me, "You are in search of something too. I can see in your eyes".

"Searching for what? I am waiting for my death to come. I have no goals in my life. I was born alone and will die alone. I am that bird who was never allowed to fly, my wings were ripped off, and was thrown into a dark cage" I stated infuriatingly.

"There is a fire, a spark in your eyes that I see. It speaks louder than your words" he said perceptively.

"It's enough already! My life has nothing to do with you. Who even are you? And why did you sit here in the first place? Why am I even talking to you? You have no place here. No human has any place here. It is better you leave right this moment." I pushed him fiercely to leave but he didn't budge. "Aren't you a human too? Why are you living alone in this entire forest? You lost someone?" He interrogated. I was getting angrier by the moment. "Why are you pestering me with your stupid questions? I am not bound to tell you anything. Go away". "Calm down Satra. You are right, I am just a nobody. But since we are strangers, you can share your pain with me. Tell me what happened."

"Dhansiri, my little sister" I yelled at him with tears in my eyes. I then told him my whole life story. I asked for help but everyone was engrossed in their own happy world that those magicians had cast upon them. No one... No one came to our aid. Everyone I ever loved, I ever thought of mine just faded away. So, I left everything and settled here for the rest of my life. I despise all of humankind. Humans are ignorant and selfish who don't care about others without any ulterior motive. I am better here, with my pain and loneliness. I will ultimately die and reunite with my sister" I broke down as I spilled my heart in front of him.

The man heard my tale silently and pointed out, "Dhansiri will never come back by living like this you moron,"

I interrupted him. "What do you know about me? Who are you and who gave you the right to judge me?

I had pain since my birth. I lost everyone I loved. You are in no position to make any statement about my life decisions".

"You are a coward, a useless child who failed to protect his own sister, one who knows only to cry and blame others. This anger that you are showing me is a mask you adopted to hide your tears. This world doesn't work that way boy. If you believe something belongs to you, you should have the strength to snatch it from their hands. You can either have results or excuses, not both of them", Eldrian said.

"I was a child! I didn't have any power or support. I wish I could turn the time back to see her again. What else could I do?" I argued with tears in my eyes.

"Something better than hiding yourself in the forest waiting for death. You should have made them realize what is the definition of pain, sorrow, and suffering? They, who were laughing, are still laughing at your misery. What have you done against it? You ran away from your duties, that's what makes you miserable", he told me.

Realizations struck me hard. My head started pounding. *"I never did anything other than weeping due to my anguish. Maybe the man is correct. Those people who were responsible for our agony should pay for their sins but I am weak and powerless. How will I ever achieve this?"* I was in a rage, "You told me your name, Eldrian, right? But where have you come from? I saw you extinguishing and re-burning the fire with your energy. Just who are you? Magician? Just like them?" I asked bewilderedly.

"Kingdom of Whia, that's the only place on the Earth where people inherit the ability to perform magic. I once belonged to the Kingdom of Whia but now I am not related to that place. I have already broken all my bonds. Having too many bonds weakens us, and makes us lose our focus. Bonds are nothing but a hindrance. I started liking this darkness in my heart, and I embraced it. Once you accept, all the darkness becomes safe, havoc becomes comfort. Satra, I am just like you. I am hurt too, by the people I always thought were mine... by the people I couldn't even imagine will ever hurt me", Eldrian said.

There are a lot more questions in my head. But I don't want any answers for them right away. I spent a long time in this forest. Now, the moment has arrived. I am ready to wipe out all of them. I want them to know what it means to breathe in fear, what it means to hide in the dark, and what it means to lose every last hope that keeps us alive. I want them to feel the exact pain and suffering that they served me. "Eldrian please teach me" I begged him. "I want to become strong. No matter the consequences, I want to become powerful enough to show humanity the reality of despair and dejection."

Eldrian became my teacher. He was the only person who really understood me and my feelings those were penetrated deep into my heart. I promised to dedicate my life to him and I promised myself to avenge the death of Dhansiri.

6.

Secrets of Life

Everything went quiet and still. Harvey felt like drowning in pity and melancholy after learning about Arwel's - Satra's - doleful past. He took a deep breath and looked up at Arwel in his eyes "Satra, I am aware of how painful losing loved ones can be. I recognize how it feels when everything fades into memories. But Satra, revenge is not the solution. Even if you succeed, all you will ever discover hidden within you will be emptiness" Harvey tried to rationalise with him.

"It doesn't matter to me what you feel! You don't stand in my place. You will never understand the meaning of suffering", Arwel snarled in his deep loud voice.

"I lost my parents too. I loved them very much. Without them, each and every day is incomplete for me. And I have already spent a lot of such years. They were my everything. So, I am aware of this deep void one feels inside of him. The loss of Dhansiri has created a permanent scar in your heart", Harvey reasoned.

"You are a mere human - powerless, poor, and pitiful. I have elevated way above those feelings. Now I am numb to those useless emotions. Emotions are only hindrance to one's development. All I have right now is a goal. A goal to exterminate every single one of them who are responsible for Dhansiri's death" Satra said lifting his weapon and pointing towards Harvey. "Enough of your hollow words boy. Just shut up so that I can wipe you out in a fraction of a second".

Harvey courageously took a step ahead and gazed deep in Arwel's angry eyes "You are running but are not going anywhere. You are stuck and..."

"I don't even give a damn about what you think; not everybody deserves to know who I really am, and your criticism is directed at the person you imagine me to be". Satra said through gritted teeth, interrupting Harvey mid-sentence, "I walk over this path alone, neither you nor anybody else can change that. The way I managed my agony is a testament of my love and sacrifice for my sister. I am not looking to escape my darkness; I have learnt to stay in this abyss all alone for the rest of my life. I am proud of myself because I overcame the grave circumstances when I believed I couldn't."

"All this suffering for the wrong purpose will yield nothing" Harvey tried to make sense.

Arwel furiously dropped his weapon and plunged towards Harvey. He grabbed his neck with his bare hand, "Who decides that hah! Who decides what actions are right and wrong? Was it right when Dhansiri and I were neglected like stray animals to rot in some corner? Was it right when my innocent sister was on the verge of death and not even a single person took pity on us, treated us like taboo, like unwanted thrash which led to her death? Of course, I know I became a demon, a monster with no morals. But where were the morals of those people who call themselves as humans; who were the reason of her demise? And if I make those criminals understand true pain and distress, I don't think it is wrong. So don't even try to explain to me what is right or wrong."

Harvey spoke through his choked voice "indeed what happened with you was wrong. But if you inflict the same treatment on them then what difference will remain between them and you. The goal you have decided; to take revenge, will only satisfy your will but real happiness will never emerge from that".

Satra loosened his grip on Harvey's neck, "Happiness is subjective. I feel happiness from what I am doing. Tell me, Harvey, why didn't you try to find out what was the reason for the death of your parents? Why didn't you try to wipe out those who did this to you? Tell me what was your reason for not taking revenge? I will tell you why. Because you are a weak crippled little child who has no strength or no willpower to take a stand." He released Harvey to fall flat on the surface.

Harvey panted heavily to recover his breath, but didn't deter from his will. "Taking revenge huh... You have killed hundreds of people who must be related to others in some way or the other. The one you killed might be someone's father or mother, son or daughter, or maybe a sister. Another Satra must be out there whose Dhansiri was killed because of you. What was the mistake of that Satra? Was he the one who ruined your life? Do you have any answer to this?"

Satra argued, "There's no point in thinking about them. They never thought of me. No one came to feed me and my sister when we were hungry and slept even without a single bit of food. No one cared about our wellbeing. My dreams don't exist in the future. It is buried in history and that's where I belong too. I just hope Dhansiri gets her justice and I somehow end up with her in my afterlife."

Harvey replied, "A man without a vision is a man without a future. A man without any future will always return to his past. You are the one of those. Do you really think Dhansiri will come back? I never thought of any revenge because I was never taught that way. The Eldrian you met had wiped all senses within you. He has converted you into his puppet whom he controls on his fingertips. He manipulated you in believing the nonexistence of true peace and love. You are just another one of his weapons he is using to achieve his treacherous goals. Revenge was never the solution Satra. I never avenged the death because I am the reflection of what my parents taught me. My personality was built by them. They reside within me, deep into my heart, still today. They will never want me to do something like that."

Satra was left speechless. He started contemplating his life and actions till now. He lowered his eyebrows and looked down with self-realization. He realized something was erroneous, something based on wrong information. But this questioned everything that he learned since his childhood. *"Did I walk over the wrong path for all these years? It can't be. Everything I believed to be right since all this time is not the way it should be? Was it Eldrian pulling the strings all the time. No, no, I am my own person, right?"*

Harvey observed that his words are working hence he continued "hatred can become an inspiration for the evil but never the strength of positivity. You have gained so much power, why not use it for a better purpose. Let's assume you achieved in seeking your revenge. What next? What will you get? Will it bring Dhansiri back? Will it bring you the love you long for. Will it give you the true happiness that you desire? No Satra, this path leads to unending darkness. There will be pain and suffering in life in one way or another but an eye for an eye makes the whole world blind. Dhansiri lives inside you in your memories. Chase those happy memories and let go of the past".

"Does Dhansiri stay inside of me too? If yes, will she hate me for my doings?" asked Satra. It was the first time Satra felt so vulnerable and defeated.

"Dhansiri will never hate you. But I am sure she would be disappointed as you turned into everything that she never wanted you to be" Harvey answered truthfully. "But Satra, sometimes suffering is just suffering, it doesn't make you stronger. Leave this path and join hands; come with me"

"A personality is not only carved by parents; we learn from everyone in society. We were born in a very different situation. We were exposed to different scenarios and different societies. You received all the love from your mother and father. I don't know what motherhood means. I was poor, the society hated my existence and they were the reason for Dhansiri's death. They snatched every little happiness from my life. Tell me do you still believe I could have landed at a better part of my life?" asked Satra desperately.

"You only focused on what society did to you and were blind to your father's love. You lost your sister and you ran into the woods, your father lost his both children. Have you ever thought where your father is? How he is? What situation is he facing? You could have stayed with him. Whatever he was doing he was working hard to feed you. It was your responsibility to show him the gratitude and love he should have received. Not only you left your father but you killed many more fathers. The hunger for revenge made you blind", Harvey explained.

Realisation dawned upon Satra. He comprehended that all he did in all these years was fallacious. *"What have I done? It is too late to turn back to Satra. I am entangled in this curse of 'Arwel' forever. It is all over"*. He felt his heart and soul burning in sorrow equivalent to the hundreds of pyres that were burnt because of him. All that remained was a hollow body.

7.

Return of Evil

Satra fell down on his knees in front of Harvey. He was consumed with regret and grief, "I cannot cry anymore. My tears are all dried up. I feel like I have lost something. Something very important, that defines us as human beings. I have lost my humanity". He realized the mistakes he had made throughout his life. The acrimony and sorrow he has spread into the world was now approaching him, swallowing his own heart. He felt hollow and broken. He was no longer the evil that the world used to fear, the demon inside him slowly diminishing into nothingness. Deep down he was just a small child who was in search of harmony. He was no longer Arwel, he was Satra, and he always had been Satra. As 'Arwel' vanished so does his force of demonic creatures. The beasts which were the descendants of dark magic, disappeared into thin air, the darkness gradually subsiding.

Harvey turned to Satra and knelt down to hold his hands. "Welcome back Satra", he said, smiling gently with happiness. But the happiness was shattered in a single moment when a strong cataclysmic beam of light struck the Earth. The ground tremored with its impact. When the light settled, a man dressed in an off-white-coloured chiton appeared with long frizzy hair that startled everyone present there. His demeanour was intimidating, his mere presence screamed horror, so much so that even Satra seemed terrified.

"Eldrian" Satra gasped with a meek voice. His face paled out, his blood running cold.

"You have always been weak. You have failed to meet my expectations. Not that I had any high expectations from you anyway. You were a kid back then and you still are one." Eldrian hissed.

The deep gravelly voice of Eldrian was petrifying. Harvey could never imagine that the mere presence of a person could be so dreadful. A frightening aura enveloped the surrounding making everyone have their hearts in their mouths.

"It was my mistake. I should have eliminated you the day I first met you," Eldrian tutted, "that might have ended the so-called fatuous feeling of emptiness in your heart that you always babbled about. You have always wallowed in baseless feelings. That's what made you so incapacitated. I hate surrounding myself with losers. You were always a loser still I gave you one opportunity but you disgraced me. Now, you will die."

Eldrian lifted his hand and was about to strike Satra with his magical power when Harvey came in front to save Satra.

"You have to go through me. No one should touch him" Harvey was shaking in his boots but still tried to defend him.

Satra was stunned by the action of Harvey. "Why...Why do you want to save me? Let me die. I have committed so many sins".

"You will have to live and atone for what you have done", Harvey said to Satra. Satra was touched by Harvey's kindness which he felt was undeserved. Tear started flowing from his eyes involuntarily. No one had ever showed empathy towards him throughout his life. Harvey's actions even after knowing his grave deeds, moved his emotionless heart. "Such a beautiful and sweet display of affection! Amazing! This brotherly union is making me cry and vomit at the same time", Eldrian commented, sarcasm dripping from his words like venom. "What a waste, this display is futile since you both are gonna die the very next moment, by my hands of course. You are perfect for each other, both being the ultimate weaklings. Let me assuage your miserable lives by ending it!" he roared.

Eldrian being an Orabelle was the holder of a Talisman. He pulled his sword out of thin air that blazed into a blue-green flame. He bombarded Harvey with his powerful spell that was so strong that the ground exploded due to the intensity that the Talisman inherited. Harvey closed his eyes in fear anticipating his end.

But it never came. He opened his eyes gently and found Reva shielding him with some sort of magical force field. She stopped Eldrian's attack to save Harvey.

Eldrian laughed bitterly, "Oh Reva, so it's really you. I thought you had died during the disposal of the Kingdom. I never thought you would come back and dare to stand in front of me like this. Just look at you, how old and frail you have become. You are fragile and debilitated just like my younger brother Ezra. You are weak just like him who was never fit to the throne. It was always me who was supposed to be rightfully entitled as the ruler of Whia. I just don't understand what Father found in him because all I could see was his incompetent, amateurish, and useless behaviour, like a coward who always hesitated in making decisions. The loss of Kingdom was the spoiled fruit that was planted by father himself".

"All I know is that you have been the reason for the loss of our Kingdom" Reva retorted angrily. "I will avenge you for not only our homeland but also for the loss of those lives that were my responsibility. It was your doings that I lost my people, my love, and my kid. You killed a mother that day!" she shivered with rage. "Now you will pay for your sins". She took her staff and knocked it twice on the ground. The bamboo staff transformed itself into a wand from the bottom to its top. The wand was beautifully carved with a precious gem at his tip. The tip glazed with a bluish-green flame similar to Eldrian's sword. "I am a descendant of Theo Orabelle as well. You will have to face my Talisman here and now".

Listening to this, Eldrian laughed mockingly, "Face you? You cannot even touch me. Don't you know who I am? I am Eldrian Orabelle. I am the strongest Talisman holder. I am unstoppable!" he boasted proudly.

"Enough of your words", said Reva and attacked Eldrian with a blow using her wand. Eldrian slashed it with a single flick of his wrist. The fight began and both were striking each other with full power. Not only Harvey but Satra too found it to be astonishing yet threatening. The power was strong enough to slit the Earth into halves. Eldrian charged an intense strike towards Reva. She managed to dodge it barely but the energy wiped out nearby land. "This is the real power of Talisman," Satra said, staggered with the ongoing exchange of onslaughts "I foolishly followed the cursed path to be the holder of such power, but the truth is, I can never wield it."

Reva held her fort with all her might. However, Eldrian was too tough for Reva to handle. The assault of subsequent powerful blows was beyond her capacity. She fell on the ground, defeated and lost. The incident shocked both Harvey and Satra and they stood rooted to the ground. "Reva, you poor soul, did you really think you could stand a chance in front of me? A

The True Talisman

Talisman that has been born with you, grows strong with you and as you turn old, it turns old too and when you die it vanishes along with you. Your Talisman was weak because you are feeble and decrepit. I will make sure that you are counting your last few breaths here. You are dead", said Eldrian.

"W-What have you done to yourself? From where does all this power come? You are my uncle, your Talisman should have been weaker but it is as if its strength never deteriorated. What is the source of such strength of your Talisman?" Reva asked in her fragile exhausted voice.

"You are so naive Reva. The path of true strength goes through the darkness of purgatory. I earned this power with all my heart and passion to pursue my dream of eliminating every last one of Ezra's bloodlines. You want to know the source, huh. Guess I can tell you since you are on the verge of your end. I cursed humans and devoured them myself to attain this strength. Their life source is indeed potent enough to bolster my Talisman", Eldrian revealed his secret. "Enough of your words now. I want you dead", by saying this Eldrian lifted his weapon with one hand and pulled Reva with her hair using another. He mercilessly slit her throat right in front of Satra and Harvey and the blood slowly stained the battleground.

"No! No! No! You cannot do this to her", Harvey screamed while he sprinted toward Reva.

"Harvey stop. He is too strong." Satra tried to stop him. However, his words fell on deaf ears. Harvey kept running toward her. He reached to her side and took her, now just her remains as a corpse, in his arms. The sight was gut wrenching. Harvey's words stuck in his throat. He just wailed in sorrow, the memories of Reva saving his life multiple times, the people and his experiences in this small magical world in such a limited time reeled through his mind in an endless loop. In the minuscule time he spent there, he was deeply attached with everyone through their stories. His very life was a gift by Reva and now he was helplessly carrying her corpse, unable to save her. "I am sorry, I am so so so sorry I couldn't save you" was all Harvey could muster.

Eldrian laughed like a devil incarnate... "Finally! Finally, I have made my dream come true. Every single one of Orabelle dynasty has vanished. I killed them all", he revealed with joy. He then glanced at Harvey sobbing with Reva lying in his arms.

"Harvey... Have you learnt your lesson yet? The weak will perish by my hands. Only the strong and ruthless will survive. Now let me predict your future for you. First, this useless piece of thrash will die" he pointed towards Satra "and then it's your turn. It will be quick and painless, just like I killed scores of other humans. You will be the part of life source of my Talisman, at least that will make you useful for a change", Eldrian said.

Harvey was stoned listening to this, "What? What did you just say?"

"Yes, you heard right. Humans are mere weaklings, valuable only as soul-suppliers, strengthening my Talisman. But Reva wasn't even worth that I tell you. Just a soul-less lifeless corpse. She deserved to die." Eldrian laughed boisterously.

Harvey saw red. The anger now has taken the form of wrath. He lost his consciousness and stood up to run towards Eldrian raising his fist to attack him.

Eldrian watched Harvey approach him amusedly. He lifted Harvey in the air with just a movement of his finger. "You can't stand in front of me. I don't understand why you even try", Eldrian tossed him away like a mere bug.

Harvey fell on the ground, with a loud thud and couldn't breathe. Eldrian laughed at his state "What were your teachings to Satra? What did you tell him? Not to take revenge and all. Look at you now. You humans are so pathetic who cannot even stand by their own words."

Eldrian reached towards Satra. He grabbed him by his neck, chocking him violently. His body being lifted a few inches above ground. "And you were supposed to be my little pawn. But you went ahead with your woeful self and suddenly followed the path of saints. What do you think you deserve?" Satra gagged and whispered "You are right I deserved death. I feel like I don't belong anywhere. You can just kill me". Harvey, knocked away, was on the brink of unconsciousness and was lying next to Reva's Talisman. He was so severely hurt that his body went numb and torpid. He could not move a muscle. A couple of his ribs were broken and he couldn't lift one of his legs, surely fractured. He opened his eyes partially to see Reva's Talisman disappear. The Talisman started to vanish as it gradually turned into ashes which were an indication that Reva Orabelle was no more. This hurt Harvey more than his wounds. He remembered; she had called him their savior. *"I fail to live up to the expectations of people who believed in me. She was wrong. How can I be a savior when I couldn't even save the only person who saved me multiple times?"* Harvey closed his eyes questioning himself as well as accepting his fate and defeat. A thin trail of smoke that appeared from the remains of the vanishing Talisman reached Harvey and found its way to his heart. Now, all of a sudden, his heart started beating so fast that it would burst out of his chest. A magical aura appeared, surrounding him like a cocoon as he regained his consciousness. He felt the vigorous stream of energy running through his nerves. He pushed himself to stand on his feet. "Do not even dare to lay a finger on him or you will regret each of your life's decisions" Harvey's raucous command echoed in the periphery.

"How are you still alive and standing on your feet? You should have been dead by now. I have not grown weak now, never had. This is just a fluke which won't happen twice!" Eldrian seethed while he capriciously threw Satra down and approached Harvey like a lion advance towards his prey. "You should have known by now that you don't stand a chance in against me without a Talisman. But an inutile human like you won't learn your lesson without being annihilated for good. To fight a Talisman possessor, a Talisman is required, where is yours?"

Harvey took a step back and then dashed into Eldrian with his full vigour. The force of the blow took both of them flying in one direction. Eldrian tried to draw and summon his Talisman but Harvey was too quick this time. He caught him off guard at the right moment and barrelled him away.

Eldrian was drastically hurt and at the same time was appalled by Harvey's new found capability. "Who are you?" he asked while lying on the ground.

"I am the Talisman" the glorious voice of Harvey echoed like a heavenly sermon.

Talisman was a powerful weapon and could take any shape and form. This was the first time it appeared in the shape of a human soul. Harvey then lunged towards Eldrian using every bit of rage stored in his body. He showered a barrage of blows on the elder one but he wasn't one to back down easily. When the next attack from Harvey came, he held the assaulting fist instantly and pushed him away with all his might, the later still holding his stance intact at a distance. Eldrian was furious. He charged with an ugly sneer dripping hateful venom likely planning to barrel him over. Harvey let him close in, and at the act moment, he shifted and flipped him through the air before slamming him into the ground. It knocked the wind out of him and Harvey didn't let him recover and twisted his arm behind his back. His options were to surrender or risk breaking his arm to get free. He was covered with his own dripping blood. He strainingly rotated his neck to glance at the impending yet familiar doom hovering over his entire being. "Father, Is that you?" Eldrian whispered with disbelief as he looked in the eyes of Harvey. Harvey possessed the same fire and aura of Theo Orabelle in his eyes. "Your end is here." With these final words Harvey landed a powerful blow encompassing all the strength of Talisman. Not even Eldrian could have survived such humongous attack on a point-blank range. He met his end, his bluish-green-flamed Talisman extinguishing and turning into ashes.

Harvey collapsed instantaneously. He fell down on his knees. "Harvey, are you alright?" he barely recognised the voice. He saw a blurred figure of Satra appear in front of him. Satra lifted Harvey into his arms. "Let's get out of this place." Harvey wanted to see his friends who were locked up in the cages but was so worn out that his eyes couldn't stay awake. He could feel the warmth of Satra as he walked him home.

The motion of Satra walking down the path resonated with a different feeling and slowly changed to something else. Somehow, it felt more realistic now. Harvey could hear the rhythmic sound. The sound of a train running over the tracks while his eyes were still closed. He woke up with a gasp and found himself seated in his place. Startled, he began looking here and there. He rubbed his eyes his few times and checked again but couldn't believe what happened. His head was dizzy. He hit his own head a few times with his fist. *"Was it just a dream?"* he asked himself. He looked at the faces of his co-passengers who were around him. The train slowed down as the station was close by. Harvey was still contemplating his entire existence when a man rested his hand over his shoulder. The man wore a brown suit and a kind smile on his face. Harvey saw his face and felt the familiarity but couldn't put a finger on it. The man gestured him, "Mister, the station is near. It's the last stop of the train. You have reached Kolkata". Harvey was baffled even more after hearing that and tried to question the person but the man went a few steps ahead in the compartment. Harvey tried to approach him but he started taking his luggage and talked to a girl beside him. "Come on Dhansiri, we have reached home", the man said. Harvey couldn't believe his eyes and ears. They were Satra and Dhansiri in front of him. He felt content, his eyes watering a little. This was the first time he saw Dhansiri. She was really pretty. Harvey got off the train with a smile on his face but his thoughts were all over the place.

As Harvey was on his way, he saw an old lady at the end of the street. She was old but her face was glowing. He was unsure whether these people were real or a mirage of his mind. He went to the lady "Are you Reva?", Harvey asked uncertainly. She smiled at him "Yes, Harvey, and I want to thank you for whatever you did", Reva said, her words were filled with gratitude. Harvey took a relieved breath, now confident that he wasn't going mad. He held Reva's hand in his. "I am so happy to see you alive. But I don't understand what is happening here. What happened to me? I saw Satra and Dhansiri a moment ago but how is this possible? And what happened to Eldrian, and the others?" Harvey was heaving at the end of his monolog.

"You just keep questioning huh Harvey", Reva laughed and continued, "In our world you have always possessed the power of chronokinesis dormant deep within you, which surged into enormous power as it coupled with the Talisman. You changed everything. You brought Dhansiri back to life. You blessed the others from Whia with life and everyone's alive. I am alive too. I thank you for everything from the bottom of my heart. You really are our savior."

"But what about Eldrian? And why is everyone so, for the lack of better word, normal like humans? Where is the magic?" Harvey enquired.

"He was killed by his own deeds. And all of us from the Kingdom lost our powers. We are just normal humans now with no magical powers. I lost my Talisman too. I guess Theo took it all back from us as it was our magical powers and the legacy of Talisman that were the root cause of all this", Reva explained and continued, "I guess Theo did what he said. He came back from death in the form of Talisman that was coupled with you during the battle. There's something in you that made this happen."

"But there are still tons of questions in my head. I am still unsettled about what is real and what has happened in my mind. Was I chosen for this? Do I still possess the power?", Harvey kept on asking without a break.

"Well, not all questions can be answered. So let go of them. Just remember Harvey, Talisman presents itself only to those who are worthy of it and believe in themselves. And I believe it presents itself irrespective of the origins of the bearer; not limited to Orabelle. Talisman is not just magic, but when you believe in yourself it becomes your Talisman to achieve anything in your life. Remember now you are the Talisman possessor. Believe in yourself and success will be with you like your shadow", Reva Orabelle patted his shoulder and started walking on her way with a smile and a feeling of contentment on her face.

"We will meet soon", Harvey said with a smile as he, too, went on his own path.

**************THE END**************

Milton Keynes UK
Ingram Content Group UK Ltd.
UKHW021120201124
451264UK00017B/326

9 789362 615466